EGMONT

We bring stories to life

First published in Great Britain in 2007 by Dean,
an imprint of Egmont UK Limited
239 Kensington High Street, London W8 6SA

Thomas the Tank Engine & Friends™

CREATED BY BRITT ALLCROFT

HiT entertainment

ISBN 978 0 6035 6259 4
5 7 9 10 8 6
Printed in Singapore

Dunkin' Duncan

The Thomas TV Series

DEAN

Rusty, Rheneas and Skarloey were helping Duncan with an important job at the Incline Railway.

They enjoyed working there.

They liked the clever way the loaded trucks rolled down the incline, pulling the empty trucks up.

Duncan didn't like working at the Incline Railway.

He was always in a hurry. That made him careless and got him into lots of trouble.

Rusty hoped Duncan would stay out of trouble today.

"There is a lot of work to do," huffed Duncan to the others. "So collect your trucks and be quick about it."

"Bossy boots!" chuffed Rheneas.

"Pushy puffer!" said Skarloey.

They didn't like Duncan telling them what to do.

Rusty, Rheneas and Skarloey were happy pushing empty trucks up to the steep incline and hauling loaded ones away.

There was a lot to do. The empty trucks were hitched to a steel rope.

Loaded trucks at the top of the incline were hitched to the other end of the rope.

Then the loaded trucks rolled down and pulled the empty trucks up.

Duncan wanted everyone to work faster. "You're as slow as snails," he grumbled.

"We're proper engines," Rusty huffed, crossly. "We follow the rules."

"We can't send up more than four trucks at a time," chuffed Rheneas.

"I'll show you how fast a Really Useful Engine can work!" said Duncan, impatiently. He banged one truck into another. And then another.

Soon, Duncan had a row of trucks. "Nothing to it," he boasted to Rusty.

"Those trucks will pay you back," warned Rusty. "Trucks don't like to be banged and shoved!"

"I can handle trucks!" cried Duncan.

Rusty could see Duncan was not going to listen. He trundled away with his trucks full of slate.

Duncan was so impatient, he became even more careless.

"I'll show that smelly diesel and those lazy steamers," he said to his Driver.

Duncan didn't notice his chain was tangled in the coupling of the truck in front of him. Suddenly, he was being pulled up the track by the empty trucks!

"Bouncing buffers!" Duncan cried. "It's got me!"

Duncan's Driver jumped clear.

Rusty, Rheneas and Skarloey returned with their empty trucks to see Duncan being pulled up the incline.

"I tried to warn him," said Rusty. "But he never listens!"

The chain pulling Duncan's trucks couldn't hold the weight. It suddenly broke!

Duncan whizzed backwards down the incline.

"Help!" he yelled. "I can't see where I'm going!"

He was heading straight for the buffers!

BANG! Duncan crashed through the buffers and landed in the muddy mine pond.

"Glug glug glug," he said. "Gluggle gluggle glug!"

No one was hurt. But Duncan felt very foolish, and very wet.

It took a long time to rescue him from the pond.

When The Fat Controller arrived, he was very cross with Duncan.

"You have not been a useful engine," he said. "You have caused confusion and delay. And you owe these engines an apology."

"I'm sorry," Duncan said to Rusty, Rheneas and Skarloey.

"Once you have been repaired," The Fat Controller said, "you will work here alone until you learn to be patient and careful."

"Yes, Sir," said Duncan.

He didn't want to fall into the mine pond again!